Cover designed by John Andrew

This book is a work of fiction. Names, characters, places, and incidents either are products of the author's imagination or are used fictitiously. Any resemblance to actual persons, living or dead, events, or locales is entirely coincidental.

John Andrew

Printed in the United Kingdom

First Printing: Aug 2018

ISBN : 9781980732426

John Andrew

FORWARD

There are various reasons why people work in mental health and It takes all kinds. Working in mental health is working with people. Dealing with the mind is dealing with life. Who is more qualified to do that than us. The following reflective fiction is for people who work in mental health, but I hope the rest of the people reading can understand where this is coming from.

This micro book is a fist bump, a hand shake of camaraderie. It's relevant to us mental health professionals but it's also relative. When I say professional I mean all that exist in the services of mental health across the globe. If you aim your perspective accurately mental health becomes less of a department of work, it becomes a way of life.

CONTENTS

THE ACTING MANAGER.

I beep myself into the Crisis team service and cautiously crawl towards my office, praying to not be informed of anything horrific regarding service users. Gina the nurse in charge tells me with seemingly great joy that one of the service users has self-harmed but are refusing to go with the paramedics to receive medical treatment. After dragging my wounded self, further down the corridor I sit behind my large oversized L shaped desk and think "I hate management."

I had been talked into an acting post by my current manager! Due to the size of the team, they needed two middle managers, they only had one! There had been other people whom had accepted the job but never made it to the post. At the last minute, they had pulled out. Much to the distress of the current manager Yvonne. One morning in the clinical meeting Yvonne received an email notifying her that the approaching lamb to the slaughter had pulled out. She read it and her face went pale. As an intervention to another human being, whom needed desperate help, I offered to be the acting manager. I was already helping doing audits and attending meetings but now I had thrown my hat in the ring. After a surprise telephone conversation from the assistant director I was acting up with immediate effect!

The NHS can do anything it wants … when it wants.

My co manager had been slowly crumbling under the pressure as she had been working for months on her own. This was a busy crisis team of at times up to sixty clients and thirty staff! That's a case load of ninety! I thought that I could give it a go with the help my melting colleague and possibly make some changes. Two weeks in all I had witnessed from my colleague was her stress.

"You know I don't sleep John I'm always working at home I never get stuff done."

"The staff rota is due, the shifts need to be released for payment. I need an admin PA to go through my emails...

"This staff member is so difficult this person has this situation... Ohhh God I moan soo much don't I? Do you think I moan too much? I think I'm toxic."

"No," I'd lie. "you've been here on your own a long time."

I was being nice to a lady who had been left alone by management for too long. Unsupervised and over exploited, now she had someone else to work with another captive. It was like she had been in isolation for years with no one to talk too. Once our office door was shut the stress would fall out of her brain and on to my lap. She couldn't stop her incontinence of speech. I'd would just absorb it! Staring amazed and scared shitless at what I might become.

"You're really selling this job to me Yvonne!" I said worriedly.

"Ohh I'm only saying…. you should go for the permanent post you'd enjoy it."

For the first few weeks things went well we worked together. Efficiently, implemented some good ideas. The handover was more organised, the multi-disciplinary team meeting happened, the case load was managed. The doctor saw people and the staff behaved themselves. I felt that we had almost achieved something. The following day Yvonne came in and started making noise about annual leave about needing a break. I understood. I even encouraged her to take some. After a stodge heavy lunch which was the kind of comfort food that she liked to indulge in, she returned and announced that she was "taking a few weeks off."

"Call me if there's any issues." She yelled as she waltzed out the door. She left early that day and suddenly I was in the office alone and responsible for the sixty clients and thirty staff! Come Monday, I'm sitting in my office with the door shut. It was one thing being the acting manager backing up the actual manager, but the acting manager was now on his own and It was weird.

Staff look at you differently. People whom had never even spoke to me before were suddenly interested in what I had to say. They smiled at me. They laughed more easily at my jokes. I wasn't sure if I liked it. If you step into a management position from being part of the team. It's an odd feeling. There's an element of paranoia on both sides. You're acting up, so you could go back within the team. You're frightened of being too managerial or too soft. You imagine people saying

"Ohhh he's changed,"

"Oh yeah who does he think he is?"

Management seemed at times like a game of emails. You receive a lot of electronic communication. Telling you to investigate this, circulate that, make sure you're using this in the care plans. Audit the whole caseload by tomorrow the commissioners need targets. The Care Quality Commission are coming soon. Please make sure you receive a good review.

Then there's the Rota, the agency time sheets the releasing for payment. The emails – "Can you make sure you send my petrol for payment as I'm struggling to survive without it." Said an angry support worker.

Suddenly you're the parent. People you've known for some time start behaving like children. Telling you "well I haven't got time to do this."

"How am I going to be able to complete this paper work when I've got to see this number of clients?"

"This person sleeps on nights and I've been telling management for ages and she does nothing about it…"

Come Friday of that week the full effect of being a manager has landed crushingly on my shoulders. I casually snuck out for a cheeky relapse cigarette when my ever-ready bad news deputy knocked on the window hailing me urgently back into the building. I stared at her psychotically and took a long drag. I wasn't even back through the door when Gina gladly informed me that one of the service users were dead! She said the word dead with her usual seeming joy. As a mental health nurse when someone tells you, a service user is dead. You metaphorically shit yourself. You go cold with pale faced anxiety and say, "fuck how?"

You run through every time you've met the client and everything you've written in the notes of the client. Then you remember "oh shit I didn't refer him to psychology. I didn't sort out his personal independent payment form and quite clearly that's why he's dead." You then run through all the seniors that will lick their lips at the thought of you getting struck off from the investigation, the coroners court and the disciplinary hearing. This all happens within five seconds. I step outside to relapse a second time.

The service user's partner had called the crisis team and informed us that her partner had died "killed himself with heroin." As both clients had addiction issues we couldn't be sure. You can't take someone's word for it when they drink six litres of cider a day. The deceased service user drank a similar amount but also used heroin and crack. He also experienced depression. But once you get that heavy into the substances, mental health services couldn't give a shit if you were Harry Potter previously, now you were an awful junkie and that is all.

To be fair he had engaged with us well, we had some good nurses with addiction experience and being in a crisis team, we were not that judgmental, we will take you into the service and engage with you. Albeit for a short time but no one's perfect.

We went out to visit, a cold call. No one was in, so the staff called the police they again confirmed that the person was deceased. They said they have been at the address before and ambulance had taken the person away. So now the staff start to fester. Gina begins to look at the notes she performs an impromptu name and shaming of all staff that saw this client last. Hoping to find all staff she hates and bury them under and heavy blanket of guilt. Staff are instantly infected by the toxicity and joy of scandal.

Great! First week on the job and we had a possible suicide. I'm not even the actual manager and now I'm going to be suspended for running a shit team. I take the leadership role and speak to staff try and settle the nerves. They appreciate it, but then scurry of in corners to check their own involvement with client. At this point, everyone is under suspicion all will be guilty by association. Gina was trying to implicate everyone!

I call the coroners to see if the body has come in yet. They report that the body must have gone to another area or it's on the way. I go outside to smoke. I wasn't relapsing any more that's a lie. I was back to ten Marlboros a day, since Friday. I spark up. Just as the nicotine hits the brain the assistant director pulls up in her Range Rover gets out and totters forward on her exec heals.

"Hi John." she greets me with the smile of a sent assassin. When you've finished let's talk inside shall we?" She muttered. I suck hard on the cigarette hoping to find the heroin in tip.

Inside she does a nice read through of the engagement. She runs down the public and political sensitivity of the situation. She notices that on the night before he died that he called the crisis team. She notes that he was told that the 'there was no capacity' to come out this late. She questions me on this. No cigarette contains enough heroin!

She needs to explain things to these nurses and this might mean them not coming to work till she meets with them next week. Just to make them aware of the risks and concern of their practice. Protecting the organization and all that…

"Did you call the coroners court?" she demands

"I did … they aren't aware of it."

She makes calls and people are partially suspended. (I hear you, how can people be partially suspended...well they can if the Assistant Director wants you to be) I fucking hate management!

I sit in the office depleted. Rock Bottom. The phone rings. It's Yvonne the actual manager. Incredibly she tells me she has been too stressed, too toxic in her personal life and work to continue in the job. She has heard the bad news on the grape vine.

"I've gotta go.. sorry it's been good working with you but I've had enough .. I've resigned." She whispered. Resigned! The penny dropped. She just wanted someone to hold the wheel as she jumped out of the speeding car. Like Oswald I been left with the smoking gun. I go outside to relapse a third time. I turn and again glare mentally at Gina whom was looking in my direction. She rolled down the window. Again, I glared at her psychotically trying to get as much buzz from the cigarette, still no opiates. I could feel my blood pressure increasing I was getting the pain under my arm. Gina shouted at me again through the window.

"You are smoking way too much mate! Anyway, good news the police fucked up. That guy is not dead! He took an intentional heroin overdose he's on the general ward!! You OK? You look pale."

I fucking hate management.

THE JOE INTERVIEW.

I first meet Joe on his day off. He has invited me to his house on the south-east coast. I drive through the town and past the harbour. Joe invites me into his modern town house and we walk through the hall into his kitchen and out to the garden, where he's made some coffee. I compliment him on his house he thanks me but adds "Too many stairs mate."

Joe is built and stocky, but you don't see him in this way. He's has a relaxed confidence that I will remember about him, and he proves easy to talk easy to, he can give you opinions on pretty much anything, before we even met in person we've talked on the phone about issues from suicide to Julian Schnabel to Trump. We sit round a rustic garden table and chairs and he tells me he's glad that I'm doing these interviews and hopefully what it will shine a positive but interesting light on his profession.

This morning he's free, his wife, a health visitor is at work and the kids are at school. Yesterday was his son's 5th birthday and he had a big party at the sports centre, from what he tells me he's glad it's over. Joe has agreed to give me some of his time, so I can get an idea of his job and a sneak peek into his working life. But there's something I want to pick his brain about first.

There's a famous story that one summer night five years ago Joe talked a young man out of killing themselves. Joe didn't know whom that person was, but he soon was informed. The story goes that police were called to a nearby bridge on a humid night in July. Joe had finished a brutal shift coordinating the crisis team and was wearily driving home. As he approached the bridge he could see what was happening, he dealt with these types of situations every day and knew that the police could manage it, but for some reason he got out and identified himself to the police and was allowed speak to the young boy.

The outcome was successful that night. The young man choose life! He went home spoke to his parents and got some help. Nothing new there. But it turned out that this kids mother was one of the trust's top board members.

Once she was told the story. It became urban legend. Joe was personally thanked in the trust paper and in person. Legend has it that he was offered pretty much any post he wanted. Joe refused pretty much whatever they offered him as he says, "He struggles to be a company man!" No doubt the mother will never forget him and what he was able to do that night. When I approach Joe about what he said that night he simply says, "I just told him to stop being such pussy!"

This I later learn is a typical response for Joe. He can switch from being the funniest guy to then having a life or death conversation with someone in seconds. He changes the subject and we jump in his Toyota 4x4 and head out for lunch ahead of his twilight shift. He lives near the beach and he takes us to a pub for a lunch. It's a glorious day and we sit on tables overlooking the water. Joe orders some surf and turf . We leave the wine of the menu, but Joe's assures me the expresso's "are mental."

Over lunch I discover that he thinks psychiatrists are bullies that ultimately like to label people. Labels which Americans made up to aid their insurance claims. "The only label that matters is the label that you give yourself." He says. When I ask him why he became a nurse and what makes him go to work every day he tells me "I haven't decided if I want to be a mental health nurse yet."

So, what about the labels? Joe's perspective is that psychiatry is about social control, not in too much of a bad way he's says, "If you knew the number of humans on medication you would be shocked." he goes on to say he feels the NHS system needs to change. The psychiatrist is becoming defunct. They diagnose, and they lend clinical leadership, that's all. Nurses are the ones trying to undo the bad engagement of a doctor. Helping them understand the label that they have been given. Which means nothing. Nurses are left out of the equation totally.

"Nurses can do all these things and better. But they want to keep paying the doctors more and the nurses less. Why? If it's about responsibility, then well I'll take a hundred grand a year for your medical responsibility. Cause it's the nurse that gets the blame at the end of the day anyway. The doctor always deflects it."

Our food arrives, and we dig in. This town has become home for Joe since he and he wife had two children. To save on the child care they moved from London back to where Joe is from. His parents help with child care and it saves him "shit loads of cash."

He says he likes a few of the restaurants but most are not as good as they think, and the prices take the piss. It can be a bit pretentious, but it suits him. Joe is somewhat of an artist himself and he and his wife paint and attempt some modern art together. They rent a pop-up stall on the harbour once a month to show and sell their art.

"It helps escape the grind as Kowalski says. It helps me gain some perspective on what I'm doing. Helps protect myself from them making me a company man."

After lunch, we head down through the high street and he gives me a guided tour of the town. We weave curiously through the art galleries, pubs, butchers, boutiques and charity shops heading towards the harbour to take in the bustle. Joe's receives a call. His team are short staffed, and they are requesting that he comes in early at four, he agrees. I will accompany him. He promises it will be fun.

Joe works at a crisis team also, a crisis team is a team that home treats clients, they assist early discharge from the ward also prevent admissions coming from the Community Mental Health Team's. Which means a lot of new referral assessments from many agencies. CMHT's, GP's and Police.

"Nowadays its mostly about risk. It's rarely just about mental illness. It's social economic factors dysfunctional lifestyles leading to a lot of suicidal ideation. Which leads to blame. In my line of work when someone commits suicide they come looking for the last person that saw them."

He seems to get distracted by something at the lights but doesn't finish his sentence Then adds ..

"You have to understand that whether you like it or not. You are representing the trust. You are representing a public and political organization that needs to protect its image."

The twilight shift can be a tough gig picking up new referrals and cleaning up mess made by the early shift, - missed visits or failed promises to clients.

We park the 4x4 Toyota outside in the yellow zone. He doesn't "give a fuck" about getting a ticket as the "cowboys can't enforce it anyway". "You go to work you wanna get a parking space."

His team are based in an acute mental health hospital. The setup is like this. Two coordinators taking referrals and organizing the visits and essentially coordinating the shift. Phone calls, emergencies etc. Joe and myself arrive we are greeted by the coordinator whom is free. The other is engaged in a what seems like a stressful conversation. The coordinator that is free reports that a regular client had been calling every fifteen minutes. Informing them that they are suicidal, low and how shit the crisis team are. Apparently, this is usual for the client.

The area of Joe's team has character. It's dysfunctional urban hills reflect the unstable mood and diverse population. Georgian and Victorian houses lead into benefits streets with oversized wide screen televisions.

The first client we experience is Clive. He has a diagnosis of Bi Polar affective disorder. Joe reports that he has had a generic relapse where he was altering his medication slightly himself without running it by his consultant or nurse. His mood became erratic, obsessed with the little things suddenly his mind fell through the floor of vocabulary and he found himself up walking down the street naked after a heated exchange with his wife.

Joe tells me "Sometimes I get this shiver this fear that my kid will suffer like that. It's not with everyone I see, it's rare but with some you get that pulverizing empathy attack where you suddenly feel what it's like for them it's ....it informs your practice or clouds it in some way."

The visit is smooth the client is and has very good insight into his situation. This will be a closure to the community mental health team. Which is trust policy. A good job done by all and text book patient flow example. The next client doesn't prove so easy.

We pull up to a ground floor flat in one of the deprived parts of town. The client's door is open. Which we both know can mean a problem. Joe takes on a laser like concentration and the UFC conversation we were having in the car before arriving at the house stops. We are greeted by a white male wearing a woolly dressing gown, and tall and wiry. Shaved head and holding a low burning spliff.

"Who the fuck is that?" he shouts.

"Hi Bill its Joe from the crisis team."

"Yeah yeah cut the bullshit, I've taken 70 units if insulin. You're lucky I'm alive cunt."

Joe understands the level of overdose. He quickly calls an ambulance and we wait with the client. The voices told me to do it Joe, didn't have a fucking choice." Bill states.

Bill has a diagnosis of emotionally unstable personality disorder, taking overdoes is a regular occurrence with his presentation. Whether it's the insulin or his medication. He seems quite with it but with the amount he has taken he could keel over any minute. He did the same last month and was in the hospital for a week. Joe takes zero chances, he will make sure when the ambulance comes he's admitted to a general hospital to be cleared.

We all sit in the lounge on Bill's couch and watch UFC. Bill smokes spliff after spliff. Joe looks over to me and gives a genuine grin of enjoyment. It's a moment where if you are not experienced you'd be shitting yourself. Concerned that this vulnerable person will be dropping down dead at any moment, he's attempted to take his own life. We are getting him medical attention the quickest way we can. All of us sitting on the couch watching UFC each person reflecting on vulnerability. Times like these you don't need to mention the obvious. We talk MMA. Bill is very knowledgeable and so is Joe. I learn a lot a lot about weight classes and weight cuts. Connor MacGregor has some punch.

Eventually the ambulance arrives, and Bill agrees to go and be medically cleared. Joe communicates to Bill that the crisis team will be with at the hospital. In the car we discuss the theories that attempt to explain personality disorder, but no one really knows. A combination of attachments issues and trauma growing up, but also the way they have interpreted their life. It manifests in self-harm, reoccurring suicide attempts and negative thought processes. Leading to a dysfunctional chaotic lifestyle.

"It's not about fixing it, it's about managing the thoughts managing the behaviour reducing the chaos in their life." Joe says.

I'm struck by the heavy nature of the job and the seriousness of dealing with these types of people. But the nurses I've met today are incredibly friendly and cheerful, insightful. Not surprising I guess considering challenging nature of the role.

The rest of the shift is classic mental health nursing. We provide back up for a mental health assessment that involves the social workers, police and paramedics. A Kenyan lady married to a British surgeon, whom becomes very paranoid and hostile when unwell. The social workers and police needed a court order to remove the person from their house as she would not engage. The husband was extremely distressed by the situation and extremely concerned about his wife. Joe sits with the husband while his wife is being escorted to the ambulance and off to hospital.

Joe listens lets the man speak. Joe gives some rational as to what is happening and puts the husbands mind at rest. Joe outlines the pathway of care for his wife. They talk risk indicators and aftercare. You sense the husband will sleep tonight but without his intervention I'd doubt he'd rest.

On the way, back to base we come up on the bridge where Joe famously talked the young boy down. It's a royal summer evening and the view from the bridge down the river is almost meditating, I can't help thinking of apocalypse now and the journey towards general Kurtz. We sip on red bulls and Joe enjoys a Marlboro, we share a moment of silence. The sun sets and as if saying 'same time tomorrow.' Joe nods to me and says

"Let's go back, if I don't write it up it didn't happen."

We climb back in the Toyota, I wonder if I should ask again how he talked that young kid off the bridge that day. Then I realize. It's between them.

A REFLECTIVE ACCOUNT.

For the last year and a half, I have been fortunate enough to talk thirty people out of killing themselves. I saved thirty lives! Which I have received no thanks for. Nothing. Not even a gift or card, from the ungrateful fuckers themselves or their families.

I spent two hours on the phone once talking a young woman out of taking an overdose of antihistamines and Lactulose. Afterwards I got criticised by the clinical lead for being on the phone too long, as it affected the response time of the crisis team and delayed patient flow.

I have also been attacked five times and spat at in the face and called a fat fucker on several occasions. After restraining a client for thirty minutes, I was suspended and investigated for unreasonable force.

I have attended many study days and feel that most of them do not help me in my every day job and are based on some kind of alternate universe where this academic shit makes sense and has a positive effect with people with mental illness. In all theories of understanding Personality disorder not one of them helps the mental health nurse deal with someone that calls a Community Mental Health Team daily threatening to kill themselves.

Now even if you are the Dalia Lama himself, if you're receiving a call from someone that threatens to kill themselves every day, even the holiest of holy's on the tenth day is going to think – hang on this person is winding me up!.... I'm gonna call their bluff. It's not that I'm being harsh or a bad mental health professional it's just human nature ...it really is. You take a deep breath and say 'let's explore why you feel this way...

The phone has rung in the middle of a busy shift, your finding a bed for an admission you're coordinating visits for staff etc. The voice at the end of the phone says 'I wanna kill myself!' Great?!

Your first thought is oh FFS! I was just about to tuck in to a nice subway 6inch and a packet of crisps now this fucker wants to tell me he's going kill himself. You spend the next hour pretending to care, try and be therapeutic and offer choices and alternatives to their pain.

But what you're really saying is

"Please don't kill yourself on my shift I don't want to write a coroner's report and then actually go to coroner's court and possibly get the sack!"

Remember this is honest reflection!

Not normal dishonest reflection. I can't reflect like this and get revalidated by the NMC, but I work in mental health and saying these things out loud makes me feel better. Why am I any different from the person on the other end of the phone? I need support too. Hearing someone tell you they are going to take their own life and then informing you that it's 'your fault' if you don't immediately come around their house to save them, Is quite distressing, added to the fact that you almost believe your trust will agree with them just to save their image.

My theory when faced with these type of situations is to promote suicide. Ok .. maybe a suicide amnesty. Suicide week. Anyone that calls reporting suicidal ideation, you encourage it. You offer support in achieving this. Reinforce motivation and methods. Explore how to properly slice a wrist to bleed to death. The best medication to overdose on. What bridges or cliffs to jump off! See how more satisfied and happy and less troubled or conflicted the staff will feel this week?

For the client this is their treatment, all the above is what feels good. This is the coping strategy. Thing is university never told you this, they never told you that this is what makes them feel great. That mental health owns an optimistic dark humour. But it does, that is what helps us breath. It makes us better. Irony is lost on most nowadays. The audience don't care if the comedian believes the joke or not. But mental health professionals do care, irony is a friend.

A GLIMPSE OF LL.

When your growing up you have dreams. LL had dreams to be an actress she was the high school actor, the lead in all productions, she wanted it. But life gives you what you need not what you want. At sixteen she finished her run playing the lead in CATS, the high school musical. She says she knew who she was. She jumped into her boyfriend's Tom's car, he was older and fast! So fast he couldn't control his car from driving through the front of a person's house on a tight built up bend. The car went through the living room window and Tom was killed instantly.

No one was sitting in the front room of the house where the car entered. LL was unconscious and injured. The slice to the face seemed to suck all confidence out of her performing life. She didn't perform again until she was Twenty-five!

Today the scar on LL's face slices down her mid cheek, at first you don't see it but if the light hits her face you catch it ...before it hides again. The injury and the guilt of losing her boyfriend, the insistent bullying of her compulsive neurosis infected her. The heart that shined through her skin was now sufficiently covered in the cloak of procrastination and fear.

She would tell her mum "I'm young I'll act later in life... I'll go to drama school when I'm ready!"

LL past the time working in her father's bike shop. She enjoyed fixing things. It protected her from the world she wanted but knew that she could no longer have.

One spring morning five years later, the sun glowed through the large shop front window as her father decided to show her how to take apart a new speed racer. The pieces of the new racing bike appeared large in their shadows on the floor.

Here, she had a moment, the counselling she had after her crash, the confidence she lost, the lust to perform, instantly returned. She suddenly understood that she had been broken but knew how to reassemble herself. The thought aligned perfectly in her brain like two hands of clock striking twelve.

She saw what her father had been demonstrating all these years, ever since the crash. In fact, ever since she was little. We can get better. We can reassemble the parts to function to the best of our ability.

LL knew she would act again but she also knew she could help others assemble themselves too. From mental health nurse training to cognitive behavioural therapy to now cognitive behavioural therapy and performance. LL was hurt. Damaged. A young life taken in a second. She felt she didn't deserve dreams, she didn't deserve to survive.

"I felt I didn't deserve success." LL says. "It's very tough place to be living but not living." LL looks back at herself now. She pauses ..it just motivates her to help others out of that situation. "Change your perspective you change your world."

She admits her nursing career was a stepping stone to Cognitive Behavioural Therapy but it's given her a perspective and edge a lot of the other people in CBT don't have. Unfortunately, a lot of the psychologists are frankly quite sheltered and haven't worked with the complex clients the nurses have. They should make it easier for nurses to become CBT therapists, the NHS needs more. It enhances your practice.

LL tells me she is fortunate to have two passions now instead of one.

Later that day LL walks out on to the stage of her gig at the Duke. She's nervous and gets a few wolf whistles as she's still beautiful, the scar from the accident peeking out shyly to the audience.

Her first few jokes hit the mark and she's suddenly LL the 'stand up.' Smashing it with insightful observations of life. The high school potential has returned. Repaired and faster than before.

WARD ROUND DAY.

You're late for the seven o'clock handover and the night nurses take great enjoyment in your tardiness.

"Where almost done you'll have to check the notes for the main info." says Lucy the unhappiest nurse you could ever meet. World renown for only sleeping and medicating patients on nights but always happy to judge her fellow nurses.

Once the handover is completed you look at the diary and remember it's ward round. A time where all patients are reviewed by the multidisciplinary team. You also remember that only half of the community mental health nurses have been invited and almost all other health care professionals have not been! Shit. You look up and wonder if this ward round can be retrieved prevented from being an utter disaster and if so spare yourself from the egotistical consultant's rant about "how disorganised this ward is and that he shall be speaking to the matron about it...."

The staff don't seem too unhappy today and the ones that are here aren't to gossipy. Which means I might avoid certain issues. Some nurses live to gossip in the office and pretend they are the busiest person to ever work by doing fuck all. The ward is a great opportunity to talk all day about yourself and slag of others.

So, you look to who've you've got on shift. Jenny, a good nurse but she's going to be doing medication all morning. You've got Clive and Toni essentially crowd control. Clive is under investigation for watching porn on a night shift and he has been distracted at work ever since. Toni And Vanessa are relatively stable, and we need to be strong this morning. Now Vanessa could assist me with making the calls to the community nurses things might be looking up. Just as I do look up a chair has been thrown through the air. Hits the office window, it's Perspex so the window only wobbles. Danny bangs on the glass and screams "if the doctor doesn't let me out of this ward today I'm kicking off."

The response team are called. Clive is front line; the team arrive, and he's escorted to his bed area. Medication considered. My intrusive mind thinks if he's sedated then he won't warrant the ward round which is a bonus as his Community nurse hasn't been invited. But let's face it it's not going to solve the issues. I walk through the ward and request that Jenny can avoid medicating Danny as I hope he will be discharged. She agrees.

"Inappropriate admission anyway and mostly social economic issues. We don't need that level of disruption on the ward." Says Jenny. Peeping from behind a drug chart.

Back to the office if I catch three community nurses early they might give me grace and agreed to attend the ward round. I'm greeted by Michelle she a diagnosis of personality disorder she announces that she also needs to leave.

"Fuck me dude if I'd thrown something like that at the window I'd be on ITU! Yeah, you guys are unfair the way you treat people. If my doctor doesn't let me out on leave then I'm kicking off big time."

"Michelle everyone has different presentations please be calm I'm sure we can come up with a good plan today." I plead.

In mental health they call pleading 'de-escalating'. Michelle pulls out a half-smoked cigarette which she knows are banned gives me the finger and walks off.

"Bruvver bruvver." I turn and assume that the client is referring to me as Anan usually does.

"Bruvver I've just called my CPN they can't make it they said they didn't know about it. But it's OK I don't need that lazy cunt. I wanna stay here for a bit I like it. I fancy that Vanessa she's fit. I think I'm in!"

"Ok Anan I'll speak to the doctor."

The ward round is almost a success the Community nurses that attended pretended to know their clients even. The clients were granted leave from the ward and no one really protested about their clearly awful treatment from the hands of stressed out nurses and ignorant psychiatrists. Anan was very impressive in his quest to stay longer on the ward. He knew he was well enough to go home and but had been previously deluded enough to exploit 'delusion' and get away with it. He outlined with sophisticated rational how he felt that Vanessa was in love with him and pointed out several occasions where he could evidence this. He got another week. He was pleased with himself and his finale was to announce to the consultant that he 'could see the intimate way he made eye contact with the pharmacist'. The consultant went bloodshot with embarrassment. It wasn't common knowledge, but they had been having an affair for a while. All staff in the room worked hard not to smirk or snort. Anan left grinning in victory.

When we leave the ward round I am immediately approached by Jenny. She looks pale and perplexed. She informs me that clients Marlon and Sue have just been found having sex in the relaxation room. I am so fucked. As I imagine my impending doom I see Danny, who had behaved earlier in the ward round but denied leave, lift the heavy wooden chair from the dining area and runs with it and propels it thought through the window smashing it clean. He kicks it out and with the agility of his hero the Indian from 'one flew over the cuckoo's nest' climbs out of the ward.

The ward awakens with an enlightened roar of exhilaration. The shiver of freedom is felt by all staff and patients in that moment. The fornication of Marlon and Sue pale in comparison but my anxiety still remembers how this will all add up in the matron and consultant's negative perspective.

Terry a gentle man with quite a chronic psychotic experience. Stands beside me while all this is happening. He nudges me out of my panic and holds my gaze. "He is you and you is he. You are a smart young man. Don't pretend you can control this. You see this" he points to the chaos occurring before us "this is not your fault."

Terry walks way and sits to observe the show. I in spirit I wanted to sit with him but decided against it. I needed to resolve the ward at least before I was suspended. Terry gave me a wake-up moment though. Let's face it. Psychiatric wards make patients of us all.

THE THERAPIST.

When Jack awakes he is present. His issues problems stresses are not present. For a few minutes in this waking moment he always feels liberated but then he would remember... Some days nothing came, apart from the greatest hits that he could just scroll through without playing, but recently there was a new release and this track he had continued to listen to repeatedly but couldn't quite get the melody.

Jack's father had died. Jack remembered that he showed love rather that said it. Which was enough for Jack. Still, Jack felt loss. He turned to observe Linda his wife. Six months pregnant. A beautiful black woman. He saw the empty glass of wine by the bedside and raised his eyes. Linda didn't usually drink but absolutely could not sleep with her large and hard pregnant stomach and the wine was the only thing that eased this. Jack loved his wife and was extremely happy the she was having his baby.

Jack a therapist, worked for a third sector group and enjoyed it. Today he had clients scheduled in also a supervision session at lunch time. His service was based in a four story Victorian town house in the town centre. He enjoyed his work and generally his colleagues. The opulence of the building inspired him most days. To some this building meant authority but to Jack it meant that some working-class men built something beautiful.

Recently Jack had felt on unsteady ground with some of his clients. He had begun to let in the intrusive thoughts more often and let sessions coast downhill. He wasn't pleased with himself, but he found it exciting and felt maybe this would lead to a breakthrough he needed.

Jack's first client of the day was Susan. Susan, a lady in her later thirties white and single. She had thoughts that were becoming too important for her. She was certain that most people found her boring when she spoke, this spread to most conversations and even on social media she was convinced people found her dull.

In the first session Jack explored the genesis of these thoughts. Susan delicately informed him that an ex-lover had imparted this information and exclaimed that she did in fact bore him when she spoke. Then broke up with her saying 'I can't do this anymore'. Like an exit interview from a disliked job.

Jack could see this, as he also felt she was boring to listen to. She had a monotone voice and rarely altered in expression of her words. Jack's job wasn't about giving her elocution lessons his job was about helping her altering her response to her negative thoughts. He could do that. Sadly, it wouldn't prevent her from being boring.

On his next sessions with Susan he was considering telling her she was boring whilst she was talking. Letting it hang in traumatic silence until pointing out the intervention. A type of 'flooding intervention' that was meant to really tackle the fear head on albeit a perverse one.

In the staff meeting he was also becoming unusually confrontational with his colleagues, almost anti therapy at times to see if he could get a reaction from his foolishly calm co-workers. Jack had become especially critical of his own cognitive behavioural therapy, extoling the benefits of no therapy and the enlightened perspective 'that therapy was ultimately a con where therapists lead clients down the garden path, milking clients out of all their cash and making them believe a reality that may or may not exist.' Being therapists, his colleagues mildly challenged him but mostly observed. They knew he would probably pick it up in his supervision. Therapist at times have dubious ethics.

At lunchtime Jack strode out of the mighty town house stood triumphantly on the wet city street. He hailed a cab and slid comfortably into the back seat. He wanted to zone out as the taxi driver manoeuvred through the city. Sat dazed in the back his phone beeped. It was his supervisor "sorry I can't make it today Jack got an emergency with a client can we reschedule?"

Jack felt a slight shiver of anger as he read it. Why is it always the clients that get the emergency? I need supervision I'm having an emergency! He stopped dazing and asked himself why? As a spoken thought did this word 'emergency' come to him. He stalled suddenly snapping out of his haze. He was instantly more alert to his surrounding whilst at the same time being distracted. Emergency. Why did he say this? Was he an emergency? Being in Jack's line of work he had the ability to overanalyze, to over think.

Jack distracted himself again and asked the cabbie to drop him at the corner. Now he had the afternoon to kill. Jack being a foodie and a comfort eater decided to take himself to one of his favourite haunts. Being that he had a good family and a what he thought was a happy marriage. He wasn't lonely. He'd always liked his own company but now with a family and busy work life the unexpected 'me time' was precious.

Jack sat in one of the newer places he knew located on a cobbled stone side street. A rustic place with Oakwood style large tables and dim lighting. Perfect for his noir mood. Jack ordered the rib eye side order of greens and a bottle of Malbec. This afternoon would be self-supervision, nothing that a succulent steak and a great bottle of red couldn't solve. Jack tore into his vices and it felt good but still free falling. He found himself scrolling through his clients in his head seeing them like a researcher going through a newspaper micro film in a library. He chooses the two clients he would see in the next two days.

Susan- everyone thinks I'm boring. Even on social media.

Clive- addicted to cheating on his wife since she cheated on him.

Jack lusted after his bloody as hell rib eye and equally bloody Malbec. Client interventions were swimming in his newly bereaved mind and for the first time in a while he felt invigorated. He ordered another bottle of Malbec. He wanted to facilitate change right now. Really facilitate change but not wait to long for it to come. Jack decided that to help his client's he should expedite their treatment. Save them some money save them some time in their life. He intended to clinically cut to the chase recognise the elephant in the room.

For once he would put the money where the mouth is. Say what the problem is. Stop dancing delicately around the issue. He will save minds. Do all the things he was trained *not* to do but always felt that he should be doing. His accredited body wouldn't approve but hey he could say he was running clinical trials. He had the plans, he handsomely cleared his plate payed left a generous tip.

Later that evening he was planning his sessions sitting at his kitchen table, his wife Jackie was in the living room. Jack's mother Pam was in the living room with her and they were doing their usual murder she wrote binge. Both women shared the same star sign and 'got on very well'. Jack believed it was always a good thing 'in essence' for a 'mother in law' and 'daughter in law' to get on.

Linda was originally from Zimbabwe, came with to England with her mother at the age of 14. Jack's mother was in her late 60's. It didn't surprise Jack that they got on so well. Linda was at times very traditional and full of common sense stability. But most importantly they liked the same tv shows. Linda loved shows like the golden girls, murder she wrote and Hyacinth Bucket. She was fascinated by the older white women. A fascination Jack didn't share. Jack was a movie and tv buff. He had time for the Scandals and the Good Wives of the tv universe- but he was more - the wire, Sopranos and Spike Lee. With that like his job came with a lacing of arrogance and patronising to the more commercial viewers.

He could hear his wife and mother discuss the decisional balance of Jessica Fletcher in a relationship with Dr Seth or Sheriff Amos Tupper. When they discussed this topic, both were unaware of how influenced they were by the characters involvement in the case. Jack usually felt this was the deciding factor for whomever they decided was a better lover for Miss fletcher. Jack having a man's mind abstained from the conversation. Jessica fletcher was best left in the relationship of solving murders in his opinion. He returned to his work. Intrusive therapy he would call it and he wrote down the beats of the intervention. Tomorrow he would begin.

Thursday Susan:

The next day Susan entered jack's office and sat. She looked unusually attractive today. Unnervingly power dressing in a pencil skirt and fitted top, heels and glasses, hair tied back. She breezed in and sat by bending her legs together and placing her rear nicely in the chair opposite Jack, placing her expensive handbag next to the chair. This was done with purpose considering her attire Jack thought. Her confidence was growing. Jack inhaled the scent of hostile therapeutic change. His present sexual attraction towards her fueled it.

Jack let Susan tell him what she had done over the last 24 hrs and how she had reflected on some of the conversations she had had with people. She began telling him about a date which she had really enjoyed but had the confidence to not agree to another date, this she identified as progress in her confidence. Just as Susan was smiling and feeling good about her choice to turn down a romantic involvement. Jack lent back in his seat and stretched fake yawned loudly exhaling

'"ooohhh I am sooo bored!" He ascended back to a sitting pose and stared intensely at Susan. Both animals stared cautiously at one another like cats following a fast howling tussle.

Clive FRIDAY:

Clive 30s of Pilipino descent. Married with two children. A recruitment consultant. He had mistakenly caught his wife cheating on him. He was out with client's when he stumbled upon his wife having a romantic dinner with her lover, whilst she was meant to be at Boxersize. She had assured him that it was now over and that she regrets the whole thing and loves her husband. Clive was prepared to forgive her but, in the process, had allowed himself, to now cheat. He had resolved himself of any guilt and rewarded himself with six months of adultery. Clive had worked quite hard around his therapy to try and figure out why he was behaving like this. Today was the day Jack would tell it to him.

Clive walked with a hunched swaying type swagger, he almost dragged his heels across the ground at points and always carried his man bag in his hand and not over his shoulder. Jack watched him walk in and sit next to him at the bar. Jack always wondered how a man with such a professional job could carry themselves like a teenager and get away with it.

Jack liked to drink in those old New York style bars. Where sitting and drinking at the bar was the norm or sitting in the booths down the side. He chooses one called Flannerys an old haunt from his training days. He could warm up the intervention with some old war stories. Clive seemed to be enjoying the therapeutic drinking session. It felt odd but whenever Jack saw uncertainty he distracted him. Jack also could feel the oddness of a professional therapy session fuelled by alcohol but felt 'fuck it 'why not. He wanted a breakthrough he wanted truth from him and his client. He waited for a glimmer of reflection in Clive's eyes. Catching him in mid boast of recent conquest then Jack fired.

"Clive? Why do you think your wife cheated on you? Clive froze. "Why do you now cheat incessantly on her? Revenge?"

Clive sipped his bourbon uncomfortably. His mind mulling over the interrogating questions. He stared for a beat pushed his glass around the table as if it were a fidget spinner. Then he returned fire

"I love my wife. I loved my wife. I was massively over weight from the age 15 til 25. I lost weight and I met my wife. We got married and here I am. I am angry because I had no confidence with women. Couldn't get laid. Women are cruel. They didn't want to be with me. They liked me, and I had plenty of female friends but couldn't get a girlfriend. I developed some fucked up ways of understanding it. When I lost weight, I began to meet women, I met Rebecca she was beautiful. I was so insecure I wasn't going to turn away from it. I felt that I deserved it I felt that she would treat me well and obviously take into consideration that I had been a fat loser for half my life."

Bingo Jack thought. Jack Daniels and coke is truth serum. Clive took another sip.

"But this was all my stuff not hers she had her own stuff people have their own stuff, for years I felt that I was the only one with issues once I sorted my shit out everyone else would be happy, the world would be happy. So, when she cheated I needed to prove my self-worth I needed to make up for lost time. What's wrong with that?"

"I'm not here to tell you that you are right or wrong. I'm here to help you understand what's going on for you."

Jack was impressed with Clive. He seemed to know why he was behaving like he did.

Across the large bar Melanie, a nosey admin girl sat for dinner with one of her girlfriends. Melanie a diminutive administrative workplace dragon Instantly spotted Jack and scanned his drinking partner through her digital database in her mind. Like Iron man's visor she found the identity and realised this was a regular client of Jacks. Even in her untrained mind she knew that this was an odd arrangement to be drinking with a client. Jack unaware of his observer, continued the intervention and in his mind was breaking ground.

Jack woke in his bed and the he felt the liberation. He felt truthful, clinically pure. He felt that today was a good day to feed back his break throughs. He turned to observe his blossoming wife. Due in two weeks Jack thought to himself he was ready to be a Father but then suddenly realised he wasn't. Jack turned away from his wife to face the other way. He hoped not from his responsibility.

In the staff meeting that morning Jack was ready and able to extol once again the virtues of his new found therapeutic style. The boss had gone around each staff member getting updates on their clients and the usual discussion had taken place. Now it was Jack's turn. Jack's boss Stewart a handsome thoughtful man with grey hair turned to Jack for a moment. He took a quick breath and turned to the team to dismiss them from the meeting.

'That's all guys thanks.'

They all awkwardly left glancing suspiciously and gleefully at Jack. Adults whom you would assume possess professional maturity lose it at the thought of another being told off. Stewart then informed Jack of admins Melanie's observations. Stewart interrogated Jack about the situations, he had received two formal complaints from two of his client's in the last 12 hours.

"One client saying that they felt that they had been put back 20 years from one of your sessions." Stewart wanted an explanation. "How's supervision going? Have you had any since your father died?"

"Err no I had to reschedule the first and the second time Tim couldn't make it." Said Jack nervously.

"Do think that your lack of supervision has impacted your perspective? Stewart now the interrogator.

Jack was lost for a response, not usual for him. Feeling the cold slice of sudden doubt regarding his new counselling style.

"Your wife is expecting soon right?"

"Err yes. In two weeks."

Stewart stared at Jack clearly thinking hard about his response and plan. Jack was again free falling.

"You've got a lot on your plate Jack. I think you need to rest, take a break. We can pick it up next week. I'll have to suspend you til I've investigated the claims. I've sent a letter to your house."

Jack's wife side stepped one step at a time down the stairs. She got to the bottom just as the post dropped through the letter box. Addressed to Jack and marked urgent and confidential. Which to a wife means 'open and read ASAP'. She read through Jack's suspension letter and gasped and rubbed her belly. The letter had either broke her waters or this was her first Braxton hick.

The intuitive detective inside her knew that this was what she had been sensing about her husband recently. Now she had it. He husband had not resolved his father's death. Had probably never resolved his relationship whilst he was alive. She knew they never had the chat. They never said good bye.

He had festered and in the style of a mental health professional that ironically is scared to say how they are. He manifested his junk in his job in his client's and now…. Suddenly the Braxton hick led to liquid on the floor at her curled toes. Linda was in labour!

Meanwhile Jack was again self-supervising in his usual haunt having another bottle of Malbec and this time a nice T bone. Rare. Half way through he was beginning to loosen up on his genius therapy techniques. Maybe it wasn't that much of a wonderful idea to simply lay on his clinical truth to people especially getting them pissed. He would have to do some professional apologizing very soon.

His phone rang it was his mum. She informed him of Linda's labour. He quickly paid and bailed on his self-supervision. Sat in the back of a taxi again dazed and reflecting on the last three weeks. The loss of his father, the break through. But most importantly realised he had not been without. He was not without now either. Linda called

"Honey."

"Are you ok sugar."

"I'm having the baby."

"I know mum called."

"Jack" Linda said. "Can you listen?"

"Yes." Jack was still.

"I've read the letter from work."

"Yes I err…"

"Jack hun. It's ok. Can I say something, and please listen…

"I'm listening."

"Your dad was very proud of you. I could see that. Your mum always tells me these things. He might not have told you but he was."

Jack was listening frozen with emotion.

"New life is coming today! Your child. So, do me favour can you get it together cause your son is gonna need you and so do i."

Still frozen but with gushing tears of sadness and joy. Jack wiped his face. He breathed in

"I will sugar. I love you. "

"I love you to. Now hurry up can you this bloody thing hurts."

Jack looked up to cab driver. Seeing his gaze, he beat him to it.

"It's ok mate I'm on it. Forget about wiping your eyes mate when that baby comes out you'll be blubbing even more. "

Jack sat back in his seat. Overjoyed that this time the emergency was not letting go lost life but bringing in new.

THE NURSES SPEECH.

We all need someone who listens. A person needs to empty their head to another at times in their life. The other person doesn't need to say anything. No grand therapeutic analytical response is needed. It's just that humans need to say what they think, what they feel out loud and not be judged or made to feel guilty or that something is wrong with them.

Try it when you're having a bad day where your favourite tunes are not deleting the madness, when the drive to work is feeling like a thirteen-hour shift, when you're so tired with worry.

Say your shit to another person don't let you eat you up! Extract it. Let it go.

Talking to each other works because of this. Say your truth out loud to another and take the world off your shoulders. It's not weakness. To know yourself, to be honest with yourself! To feel all the voices, thoughts that bombard your mind then simply walk in the direction you feel is right! This takes courage.

I helped someone today! Whether they except it or not. I helped someone.

I helped someone hopefully to help themselves. Gave them a chisel to carve out a path to go forward. I could see it in their eyes… they got it. An expanded stare of recovery. Through my words because I listened and so did they. An entwined rapport.

It doesn't always happen in the abyss of mental health revolving door frequent flyers, it's almost impossible to find a success story. Something to take you back to the beginning. To the genesis of your journey. What do I do working in mental health?

Am I making a difference. You need to find this. You need to be reminded of it.

I make a difference. I help people. Unless you become the master of your own kingdom, the organisation will abuse you like a juiced victim. But somewhere along the way helping people became a dirty word. When did it become grandiose to say that that's what you do!!

Ignore the voyeuristic nuance of modern mental health management. Of conventional pessimistic psychiatry. Just labelling and moving on productively. Meeting targets and key performance indicators.

The lecturers would say provide an unconditional positive regard, but don't inspire. Don't scream "let's get out of here it sucks."

Don't dare to say to someone "Do you want to feel better?"

I'm not jumping in the ditch with you I'm extending my hand to for you to grab. I'm not saying I've got the answers I'm saying take my hand let's get out of Milwaukie and talk about it.

Mental health professionals are like actors. You need be told you're doing a good job. You need a pat on the back. Not an analysing silence or congratulatory tick box supervision. You need resolution.

You help people!! You help people! Never forget it. Never let anybody talk you out of it.

But in the mud of the organisation you got lost. They washed your brain with the medical model and now you can't remember who you are anymore.

But today I did!

The lack of success makes a service stop looking for recovery it starts to theorise and identity targets as success because the environment for interventions isn't there. So, it's easier to say bed occupancy is down. But people experiencing mental health issues has gone up. People's unhappy experiences from mental health services has gone up. The company has pushed an agenda that saves money not saves minds.

Mental health nurses couldn't give a fuck if you save money. We want to help! If we wanted to save cash we would have gone to the city. We would have become finance geeks. Not once has a person senior to me working in mental health said you helped those clients. Not once. Clients say it all the time? Why don't we say it to each other?

The guy had anxiety he had bereavement he had trauma. He was there he wanted to get better. He needed someone to join the dots. Didn't want the magic pill bless him, he wanted to talk about stuff. I'm proud of you brother.

He believed that he could feel better, I believed I could help him feel better. I opened the door and he walked out into the world of wellbeing.

Now where's our bonus?

'

Printed in Great Britain
by Amazon